This book belongs to

_____

To my latest addition, Ben,
with love,
Daddy

First published in 2004 by Gullane Children's Books,
This edition published in 2017
by Albury Books, Albury Court, Albury, Thame,
OX9 2LP, United Kingdom

ISBN 978-1-910235-82-9
(paperback)

A CIP catalogue record for this
book is available from the British Library
10 9 8 7 6 5 4 3
Printed in China

Little Tiger's Big Holiday

Mark Marshall

We might fly on a plane,
loop-the-loop through the skies.
Then I'll need some special goggles
so no dirt gets in my eyes.

And if we're very lucky
we might zoom into space.
Floating high above the earth,
I'll need a rope around my
waist.

I'm sure I'll need a snorkel
and some floppy flippers too,
as we dive into the ocean waves
and surprise the fish there – boo!

We may just do a skydive.
Then as we drift towards the ground,
I'll need a big bright parachute
to keep me safe and sound.

I'm sure I'll need some stilts
to walk high up in the sky.
With so many amazing sights and
sounds we can watch them all go by.

We might just race each other, then I'll need a special hat. Broom broom zoom, va-va-va-voom, we'll be leaders of the pack!

And if it gets too hot,
we can run into the sea,
with Wally Whale and Zebra.
How much fun that will be!